JN244112

【改訂新版】

金子みすゞ童謡集 Songs for Children by KANEKO MISUZU

Something Nice
サムシング ナイス

訳／D.P.ダッチャー
translated by D.P.Dutcher

JULA

Something Nice

CONTENTS 目次

SONGS FOR CHILDREN

KANEKO MISUZU

translated by D. P. Dutcher

Me, a Songbird, and a Bell

Spread my arms though I may
I'll never fly up in the sky.
Songbirds fly but they can't run
Fast on the ground like I do.

Shake myself though I may
No pretty sound comes out.
Bells jingle but they don't know
Lots of songs like I do.

Bell, songbird, and me
All different, all just right.

私と小鳥と鈴と

私が両手をひろげても、
お空はちっとも飛べないが、
飛べる小鳥は私のように、
地面（じべた）を速くは走れない。

私がからだをゆすっても、
きれいな音は出ないけど、
あの鳴る鈴は私のように
たくさんな唄は知らないよ。

鈴と、小鳥と、それから私、
みんなちがって、みんないい。

Stars and Dandelions

Deep down in the blue sky
Like pebbles on the ocean floor
They lie submerged till dark comes...
Stars unseen in the light of day.
     You can't see them, still they're there.
     Even things not seen are there.

Petals drop and withered dandelions
Hidden in cracks between roof tiles
Wait silently for spring to come...
Their strong roots unseen.
     You can't see them, still they're there.
     Even things not seen are there.

星とたんぽぽ

青いお空の底ふかく、
海の小石のそのように、
夜がくるまで沈んでる、
昼のお星は眼にみえぬ。
　　見えぬけれどもあるんだよ、
　　見えぬものでもあるんだよ。

散ってすがれたたんぽぽの、
瓦のすきに、だァまって、
春のくるまでかくれてる、
つよいその根は眼にみえぬ。
　　見えぬけれどもあるんだよ、
　　見えぬものでもあるんだよ。

A Fish's Spring

New shoots of seaweed are out.
    Water's turning emerald green.

In the sky, too, it must be spring.
    Go peek and you'll be dazzled.

Uncle Flying Fish jumped through that sky,
    In a burst of light he jumped.

Hey! Let's all play hide-and-seek
    In the shade of the budding seaweed.

お魚の春

わかいもずくの芽がもえて、
水もみどりになってきた。

空のお国も春だろな、
のぞきに行ったらまぶしいよ。

飛び魚小父さん、その空を、
きらっとひかって飛んでたよ。

わかい芽が出た藻のかげで、
ぼくらも鬼ごとはじめよよ。

The Souls of Flowers

The souls of withered flowers
Are reborn, every one,
In Buddha's garden.

After all, flowers are good:
When the sun calls out to them,
Presto! They open and smile,
Give butterflies sweet nectar
And all their scent to others.

When the wind says, "Hey, come on!"
Along they go without a word.

They even give their bodies
For our meals when we play house.

花のたましい

散ったお花のたましいは、
み仏さまの花ぞのに、
ひとつ残らずうまれるの。

だって、お花はやさしくて、
おてんとさまが呼ぶときに、
ぱっとひらいて、ほほえんで、
蝶々にあまい蜜をやり、
人にゃ匂いをみなくれて、

風がおいでとよぶときに、
やはりすなおについてゆき、

なきがらさえも、ままごとの
御飯になってくれるから。

One Bee, One God

Bee's inside the flower,
Flower's inside the garden,
Garden's inside the fence,
Fence's in town,
Town's in Japan,
Japan's in the world,
World's in God.

And...and, God's inside
A little bitty bee.

蜂と神さま

蜂はお花のなかに、
お花はお庭のなかに、
お庭は土塀のなかに、
土塀は町のなかに、
町は日本のなかに、
日本は世界のなかに、
世界は神さまのなかに。

そうして、そうして、神さまは、
小ちゃな蜂のなかに。

The Sad Times

When I'm feeling sad
Strangers don't know.

When I'm feeling sad
My friends all laugh.

When I'm feeling sad
Mama spoils me.

When I'm feeling sad
Buddha feels sad.

さびしいとき

私がさびしいときに、
よその人は知らないの。

私がさびしいときに、
お友だちは笑うの。

私がさびしいときに、
お母さんはやさしいの。

私がさびしいときに、
仏さまはさびしいの。

After Our Fight

I'm alone, now,
All alone.
Oh, it's lonely on this mat.

I didn't do a thing!
She started it!
But...but still I feel lonely.

And my doll,
Now she's alone, too.
We hugged, but still I feel lonely.

Apricot blossoms
Flutter, flutter, flutter down.
Oh, it's lonely on this mat.

喧嘩のあと

ひとりになった
一人になった。
むしろの上はさみしいな。

私は知らない
あの子が先よ。
だけどもだけども、さみしいな。

お人形さんも
ひとりになった。
お人形抱いても、さみしいな。

あんずの花が
ほろほろほろり。
むしろの上はさみしいな。

By the Ditch

Saw her by the ditch.
She kept looking at the water.

Yesterday we fought.
Today I miss her.

Flashed a smile.
She kept looking at the water.

Couldn't stop smiling,
Now I can't keep from crying.

Lickety-split, run away,
Make the stones turn into stripes.

お堀のそば

お堀のそばで逢うたけど、
知らぬかおして水みてた。

きのう、けんかはしたけれど、
きょうはなんだかなつかしい。

にっと笑ってみたけれど、
知らぬ顔して水みてた。

笑った顔はやめられず、
つッと、なみだも、止められず、

私はたったとかけ出した、
小石が縞になるほどに。

The Kid Next Door

Podding, podding fava beans
I can hear
The kid next door
Catch a good scolding.

Shall I go and peek?
    No, that's not nice.
With a pod of favas in my hand
    Out I go to see.
With a pod of favas in my hand
    Back I come again.

What sort of mischief
Was he up to, you think?
That kid next door
Caught himself a scolding.

隣の子供

そら豆むきむき
きいていりゃ、
となりの子供が
しかられる。

のぞいてみようか、
悪かろか、
そら豆にぎって
出てみたが、
そら豆にぎって
またもどる。

どんなおいたを
したんだろ、
となりの子供は
しかられる。

The Clever Cherry

A really clever cherry
Thought one day in the shade of a leaf,
"Hold on, now! I'm still green,
And if these rude young birds
Peck me up they'll get tummyaches.
I'll be nice and stay hidden."
  So, hiding behind its leaf,
  The birds didn't find it,
  Nor the sun to give it color.

In time, it ripened and again that cherry
Thought to itself in the shade of a leaf,
"Hold on, now! This tree grew me.
The old farmer grew this tree.
I won't let those birds have me."
So, when the farmer came with his basket,
The cherry was hiding and
Didn't get picked.

In time, along came two kids
And again that cherry set to thinking,
"Hold on, now! They're two
And I'm just one.
Can't have them fighting over me.
I'll be nice and just won't drop."
So, at midnight when it did,
Along came a big black shoe
And squashed that clever cherry.

りこうな桜んぼ

とてもりこうな桜んぼ、
ある日、葉かげで考える。
待てよ、私はまだ青い、
行儀のわるい鳥の子が、
つつきゃ、ぽんぽが痛くなる、
かくれてるのが親切だ。
　　そこで、かくれた、葉の裏だ、
　　鳥も見ないが、お日さまも、
　　みつけないから、染め残す。

やがて熟れたが、桜んぼ、
またも葉かげで考える。
待てよ、私を育てたは、
この木で、この木を育てたは、
あの年とったお百姓だ、
鳥にとられちゃなるまいぞ。
　　そこで、お百姓、籠もって、
　　取りに来たのに、桜んぼ、
　　かくれてたので採り残す。

やがて子供が二人来た、
そこでまたまた考える。
待てよ、子供は二人いる、
それに私はただ一つ、
けんかさせてはなるまいぞ、
落ちない事が親切だ。
　そこで、落ちたは夜夜中、
　黒い巨きな靴が来て、
　りこうな桜んぼを踏みつけた。

Calves

One, two, three, four...all of us at the crossing
    Counting freight cars.
Five, six, seven, eight...eighth car's
    Carrying calves.
Sold...and where do they go to?
Only calves were on that car.

At the crossing, cold in the evening wind,
    All of us watched those cars go by.
How are they going to sleep tonight?
    There weren't any mama cows.
Where do you think those calves are going?
Where in the world are they going to?

仔牛
<small>べえこ</small>

ひい、ふう、みい、よ、踏切で、
みんなして貨車をかずえてた。
いつ、むう、ななつ、八つ目の、
貨車に仔牛が乗っていた。
売られてどこへ行くんだろ、
仔牛ばかしで乗っていた。
夕風冷たい踏切で、
みんなして貨車を見おくった。
晩にゃどうして寝るんだろ、
母さん牛はいなかった。
どこへ仔牛は行くんだろ、
ほんとにどこへ行くんだろ。

A Lightbulb's Light

Our class trip on the train that day,
   Someone singing,
      The teacher giggling.

In the evening air beyond the glass
   I saw something fizzle
      Like a sparkler going out.
It was light from a lightbulb.

I looked close and underneath
There was Mama's face.

On the train back from the hills
Someone was singing.

電燈のかげ

遠足の日の汽車のなか、
誰かはうたって居りました。
先生は笑って居りました。

硝子のそとの夕空に、
ふっとみたのは、ちろちろと、
花火のような、消えそうな、
電燈のかげでありました。

みつめていれば、その下に、
母さんのお顔がありました。

山からかえりの汽車のなか、
誰かはうたって居りました。

Song I Forgot

To this grassy hill where wildrose blooms
I come again today and think
About a song that I've forgot,
Farther than a dream and sweet
That lullaby I think about.

Oh, if I could only sing that song,
A door would open on this grassy hill
And I'd see, right here, for real,
Mama on that day long past.

Again today, I sit alone upon the grass,
Again today, look out to sea and think,
"Boat of silver, oar of gold...."
What came before? What after?
That lullaby I've forgot.

忘れた唄

野茨のはなの咲いている、
この草山にきょうも来て、
忘れた唄をおもいます。
夢より遠い、なつかしい、
ねんねの唄をおもいます。

ああ、あの唄をうとうたら、
この草山の扉があいて、
とおいあの日のかあさまを、
うつつに、ここに、みられましょ。

きょうも、さみしく草にいて、
きょうも海みておもいます。
「船はしろがね、櫓は黄金」
ああ、そのあとの、そのさきの、
おもい出せないねんね唄。

Sails

Boats that reach port
All have sails black with age,
And boats far off shore
Only bright, shining white ones.

Those boats far off shore
They never reach port.
Only the line between sea and sky
They sail to far faraway....

Always shining, do they sail.

帆

港に着いた舟の帆は、
みんな古びて黒いのに、
はるかの沖をゆく舟は、
光りかがやく白い帆ばかり。

はるかの沖の、あの舟は、
いつも、港へつかないで、
海とお空のさかいめばかり、
はるかに遠く行くんだよ。

かがやきながら、行くんだよ。

Behind the Sky

What's behind the sky?

That thundercloud can't say.
Sun's got no idea.

Behind the sky's
A weird and magic world
Where mountains talk with oceans
And people turn into crows.

空のあちら

空のあちらに何がある

入道雲もしらないし
お日さまさえ、知らぬこと

空のあちらにあるものは
山と、海とが話したり
人がからすに代りかわる
不思議な、魔法の世界です

Strange Harbor

The big clock by the old harbor
Had six o'clock at the top.
For some reason its two hands
Were moving counter-clockwise.

On the rotted and broken wharf
A single crimson flower
Swayed in the noonday sun.

On the black and still water,
Silent as a mountain,
A ship of old was moored.

In what land, what century
Is there such a harbor?
No one you ask can say,
'Cause I saw it in a dream.

不思議な港

ふるい港の大時計、
六時をうえにかかってた。
ふたつの針はやすみなく、
なぜか左へまわってた。

朽ちてこわれたさんばしに、
まっ紅な花がただひとつ、
ひるの光にゆらいでた。

黒い、しずかな水のうえ、
お山のように、だァまって、
むかしの船がかかってた。

そんな港のあるとこは、
どこのお国か、いつごろか。

誰にきいても知りゃしない、
それは私の夢だもの。

Night on the Meadow

There where cows grazed on green grass
In the light of day

    Night deepens,
      Moonlight walks.

Touched by the moonlight,
The grass again pushes up
To feed those cows tomorrow, too.

There where kids picked flowers
In the light of day

    Night deepens,
      An angel walks.

Where the angel plants her feet
There flowers open
To show those kids tomorrow, too.

草原の夜

ひるまは牛がそこにいて、
青草たべていたところ。

夜ふけて、
月のひかりがあるいてる。

月のひかりのさわるとき、
草はすっすとまた伸びる。
あしたも御馳走してやろと。

ひるま子供がそこにいて、
お花をつんでいたところ。

夜ふけて、
天使がひとりあるいてる。

天使の足のふむところ、
かわりの花がまたひらく、
あしたも子供に見せようと。

Dream and Reality

If dreams were real and real things dream,
Wouldn't it be nice?
In dream nothing's settled for good,
So wouldn't it be nice?

Night coming after day,
Me not born a princess,

Being unable to pluck the moon
Or get inside a lily,

Clock hands moving clockwise,
Dead people gone,

Nothing's settled for good, you see,
So wouldn't it be nice?
To see real things in dream sometimes,
Wouldn't it be nice?

夢と現（うつつ）

夢がほんとでほんとが夢なら、
よかろうな。
夢じゃなんにも決まってないから、
よかろうな。

ひるまの次は、夜だってことも、
私が王女でないってことも、

お月さんは手では採れないってことも、
百合の裡（なか）へははいれないってことも、

時計の針は右へゆくってことも、
死んだ人たちゃいないってことも。

ほんとになんにも決まってないから、
よかろうな。
ときどきほんとを夢にみたなら、
よかろうな。

Thin Air

A red lacquer box
Full of pretty cloth to dress her in...
　　My doll is thin air.

She's thin air, so forever and ever
Her face won't smudge, her arms won't come off...
　　She's the prettiest doll in the world.

Thin air, she is, so on top of that
She can talk and listen, too...
　　She's the smartest doll in the world.

Scarlet tie-dye, painted silk,
Changing her kimono never bores me...
　　My doll is thin air.

空っぽ

あかい手箱にいっぱいの、
きれいなきれを着せてみる、
私の人形は、空っぽよ。

からっぽだから、いつまでも、
顔もよごれず、手ももげず、
世界で一ばんきれいなの。

からっぽだからその上に、
はなしも出来りゃききもして、
世界で一ばんりこうなの。

紅い鹿の子や、友禅や、
飽かずに、飽かずに、着せかえる、
私の人形は、からっぽよ。

Blanket of Snow

Snow on top,
It must feel cold,
The chill moon shining down.

Snow on the bottom,
It must feel heavy,
Hundreds of people on you.

Snow in the middle,
It must feel lonely,
No earth or sky to look at.

積った雪

上の雪
さむかろな。
つめたい月がさしていて。

下の雪
重かろな。
何百人ものせていて。

中の雪
さみしかろな。
空も地面もみえないで。

Lotus and Chick

Out of the mud
Blooms the lotus.

It's not the lotus
That does it.

Out of the egg
Comes the chick.

It's not the chick
That does it.

These are things
I've realized.

And that, too,
I didn't do.

蓮と鶏

泥のなかから
蓮が咲く。

それをするのは
蓮じゃない。

卵のなかから
鶏が出る。

それをするのは
鶏じゃない。

それに私は
気がついた。

それも私の
せいじゃない。

The Meadow

When I go barefoot
Over the meadow wet with dew,
My feet are stained green, right?
They even smell like grass, right?

So, if I keep on walking
Till I turn into a plant,
My face, a pretty flower,
Its petals will unfold.

草原

露の草原
はだしでゆけば、
足があおあお染まるよな。
草のにおいもうつるよな。

草になるまで
あるいてゆけば、
私のおかおはうつくしい、
お花になって、咲くだろう。

Noon Recess

"Everyone playing King of the Hill, come on!"
"Everyone playing tag, come on!"

That bunch won't let me in,
And that bunch, that boy's captain.

In the shade, ignoring them all,
I draw a train in the dirt.

That bunch picked sides and started to play.
The others are choosing who'll be it.

I was feeling sort of jumpy
But now they've all begun

Through the noise I hear cicadas
Shrilling on the hill in back.

おひる休み

「城取りするもな　みな来いよ。」
「ため鬼するもな　みな来いよ。」

あの組ゃ、いれてはくれまいし、
あの組ゃ、あの子が大将だし。

知らぬかおして、片かげで、
地面<ruby>地面<rt>じべた</rt></ruby>に汽車を描いている。

あの組ゃ、わかれてはじめたな、
あそこは、鬼きめしているな。

なにか、びくびくしていたが、
みんなはじめてしまったら、

騒ぎのなかに、裏山の
蟬のなくのがきこえるよ。

On and On

I'm stepping in the light on a moonlit night when
"Bedtime!" They come and call me in.
　　(If only I could play a little longer)
　But when I go in and sleep
　I have lots of different dreams.

I'm having a good dream when
"Schooltime!" They wake me up.
　　(If only there wasn't any school)
　But when I get to school
　Friends are there and we have fun.

We're playing King of the Hill when
The bell stuffs us into class.
　　(If only there weren't any bells)
　But when I listen to the stories
　They're really interesting.

Do other kids think so, too?
Do they think like me?

次からつぎへ

月夜に影踏みしていると、
「もうおやすみ」と呼びにくる。
　　（もっとあそぶといいのになあ。）
けれどかえってねていると、
いろんな夢がみられるよ。

そしていい夢みていると、
「さあ学校」とおこされる。
　　（学校がなければいいのになあ。）
けれど学校へ出てみると、
おつれがあるから、おもしろい。

みなで城取りしていると、
お鐘が教場へおしこめる。
　　（お鐘がなければいいのになあ。）
けれどお話きいてると、
それはやっぱりおもしろい。

ほかの子供もそうかしら、
私のように、そうかしら。

Something Nice

Where the old mud fence
Is crumbling
And you see
The tops of graves...

Where in the shade of the hill,
To the right off the road,
You first see
The ocean...

Places where
I once did something nice,
I feel good
Each time I pass.

いいこと

古い土塀が
くずれてて、
墓のあたまの
みえるとこ。

道の右には
山かげに、
はじめて海の
みえるとこ。

いつかいいこと
したところ、
通るたんびに
うれしいよ。

Nightfall

My brother
Started
Whistling.

I
Bit
My sleeve.

Then right away
He stopped
Whistling.

Outside,
Night came
Creeping in.

くれがた

兄さん
口笛
ふき出した。

わたしは
袂を
かんでいた。

兄さん
口笛
すぐやめた。

表に
こっそり
夜が来た。

The Day of the Funeral

Each time I'd see a funeral,
The house decked out with flowers and flags,
I used to wish we'd have one, too.
That's what I thought till yesterday.
Today, though, it isn't any fun.
Lots of people here,
But no one looked at me.
Auntie from the city, eyes bright with tears,
Didn't say a word.
No one scolded but
For some reason I felt scared.
In our shop I was being small,
When out of the house like billowing clouds
Came a long line of people.
It's over, and I feel even worse.
No, today's no fun at all.

おとむらいの日

お花や旗でかざられた
よそのとむらい見るたびに
うちにもあればいいのにと
こないだまでは思ってた。
だけども、きょうはつまらない
人は多ぜいいるけれど
たれも相手にならないし
都から来た叔母さまは
だまって涙をためてるし
たれも叱りはしないけど
なんだか私は怖かった。
お店で小さくなってたら
家から雲が湧くように
長い行列出て行った。
あとは、なおさらさびしいな。
ほんとにきょうは、つまらない。

Goldfish's Grave

In the dark and lonely earth
What's Goldfish looking at?
  Waterweed flowers in the pond in summer,
  Flickering phantoms of light.

In the still, still earth
What's Goldfish listening to?
  The sound of drizzling rain at night
  Padding over fallen leaves.

In the chill, chill earth
What's Goldfish thinking of?
  Old, old friends
  In the goldfish pedlar's wares.

金魚のお墓

暗い、さみしい、土のなか、
金魚はなにをみつめてる。
夏のお池の藻の花と、
揺れる光のまぼろしを。

静かな、静かな、土のなか、
金魚はなにをきいている。
そっと落葉の上をゆく、
夜のしぐれのあしおとを。

冷たい、冷たい、土のなか、
金魚はなにをおもってる。
金魚屋の荷のなかにいた、
むかしの、むかしの、友だちを。

Cocoon and Grave

Silkworms
Go inside cocoons,
   Cocoons
     So close and cramped.

Still those worms, I bet,
Are really happy...
They get to be butterflies
And fly away.

People
Go inside graves,
   Those graves
     So dark and lonely.

The good ones, though,
Sprout wings...
They get to be angels
And fly away.

繭と墓

蚕は繭に
はいります、
きゅうくつそうな
あの繭に。

けれど蚕は
うれしかろ、
蝶々になって
飛べるのよ。

人はお墓へ
はいります、
暗いさみしい
あの墓へ。

そしていい子は
翅_{はね}が生え、
天使になって
飛べるのよ。

Stone

Yesterday, you made
　　A kid fall down,
Today,
　　A horse stumble.
Wonder who'll come by
　　Tomorrow?

Stone, lying there
In the country road
With the red sun setting,
　　You don't give a hoot.

石ころ

きのうは子供を
ころばせて
きょうはお馬を
つまづかす。
あしたは誰<ruby>誰<rt>たれ</rt></ruby>が
とおるやら。

田舎のみちの
石ころは
赤い夕日に
けろりかん。

Voices

At the close of day,
    when the sky lights up,
Faraway voices
    always call.

Sounds like
    Ring-a-Rosie.
Sounds like
    the waves.
Sounds like the voices of kids
    after all.

At the close of day,
    that hungry hour,
Faraway voices
    always call.

声

空のあかるい
日のくれは、
いつも遠くで
声がする。

かごめかなんか
してるよな。
それとも
波の音のよな。
やっぱり
子供の声のよな。

なにかひもじい
日のくれは、
いつもとおくで
声がする。

Wind

Eyes can't see the goatherd
Up there in the sky,

The driven goats
   at evening flock
Beyond
   the wide, wide fields.

Eyes can't see the goatherd
Up there in the sky,

The goats turn colors
   in the setting sun,
As far away
   her flute she plays.

風

空の山羊追い
眼にみえぬ。

山羊は追われて
ゆうぐれの、
曠野のはてを
群れてゆく。

空の山羊追い
眼にみえぬ。

山羊が夕日に
染まるころ、
とおくで笛を
ならしてる。

Dirt

Thud! Thump!
Dirt that's broken up
Makes a good field,
Grows good grain.

Dirt that's walked on
Day and night
Makes a good road.
Carts can pass.

You mean dirt not broken up,
Dirt not walked on
Is dirt we don't need?

No, no. That's where the flowers
With no name
Stay.

土

こッつん　こッつん
打たれる土は
よい畠になって
よい麦生むよ。

朝から晩まで
踏まれる土は
よい路になって
車を通すよ。

打たれぬ土は
踏まれぬ土は
要らない土か。

いえいえそれは
名のない草の
お宿をするよ。

Autumn

Electric lights
Each shining, each
Making shadow.
Town's
Neatly striped.

In the bright stripes
Three, five people
Wearing summer kimonos.
In the dusky stripes
Out of sight
Lurks autumn.

秋

電燈が各自に
ひかってて、
各自にかげを
こさえてて、
町はきれいな
縞になる。

縞の明るい所には、
浴衣の人が
三五人。
縞の小暗い所には、
秋がこっそり
かくれてる。

Big Catch

Red skies, sunrise.
    Big catch!
    Big catch of
      herring!

Up on the beach
    it's a carnival, but down in the sea
      they'll mourn
For thousands on thousands of
      herrings.

大漁

朝焼小焼だ
大漁だ
大羽鰮（いわし）の
大漁だ。

浜は祭りの
ようだけど
海のなかでは
何万の
鰮のとむらい
するだろう。

The Fishes

Poor fish in the sea!

Rice is grown by the hand of man,
Cows are put in the pasture to graze,
And even carps get bread on their pond.

But, oh, the fishes in the sea
Need not a thing from you or me.
They never play tricks, not even one
And still I eat them, just like this.

Poor, poor fish!

お魚

海の魚はかわいそう。

お米は人につくられる、
牛は牧場で飼われてる、
鯉もお池で麩を貰う。

けれども海のお魚は
なんにも世話にならないし
いたずら一つしないのに
こうして私に食べられる。

ほんとに魚はかわいそう。

Eyes

Our eyes,
Genies' bottles.

The orange hedge
    And the high road, too,
That cart and horse
    And the driver, too,
The buckwheat field,
    The paulownia tree,
That mountain, there,
    So far and green,
Why even the clouds
    Up in the sky,
All get small
    And all get in.

Black eyes,
Genies' bottles.

瞳

みんなのお瞳^め
魔法の壺よ。

からたち垣根も
街道も、
お馬車も、馬も、
馬方も、
蕎麦の畠も
桐の木も、
とおい、みどりの
あの山も、
まだも、お空の
雲さえも、
小さくなって
みンなはいる。

黒いお瞳は
魔法の壺よ。

Clover Field

Flowers here,
Flowers there,
Clover Field
Goes under the plow.

The plow moves on,
Pulled by a black ox
With gentle eyes.
Leaves and flowers
Go by turn
Beneath the black,
The heavy earth.

In the sky
A lark sings.
Clover Field
Goes under the plow.

げんげ畑

ちらほら花も
咲いている、
げんげ畑が
犁_すかれます。

やさしい瞳_めをした
黒牛に
曳かれて犁_{すき}が
うごくとき、
花も葉っぱも
つぎつぎに、
黒い、重たい
土の下。

空じゃ雲雀_{ひばり}が
ないてるに、
げんげ畑は
犁_すかれます。

Little Morning Glories

Once
Upon
An autumn day,

Our carriage passed the edge of town,
　　Thatch-roof cottage, bamboo fence.

On the bamboo fence there bloomed
Little sky-blue morning glories,
　　Like eyes watching the sky.

Once
Upon
A very fine day.

小さな朝顔

あれは
いつかの
秋の日よ。

お馬車で通った村はずれ、
草屋が一けん、竹の垣。

竹の垣根に空いろの、
小さな朝顔咲いていた。
——空をみている瞳のように。

あれは
いつかの
晴れた日よ。

The Mountain Pass

An evening breeze
Sifts through
Fields of maize.

Pale
Old man moon
Comes over the pass.

The pass...
Clop, clop
A tired horse

Climbs
And climbs
But only maize.

峠

夕風
さらさら
高きび畑、

白い
お月さん
峠を越える。

峠
とぼとぼ
疲れたお馬、

のぼり
のぼれど
高きびばかり。

If a Flower

If I were a flower,
A proper child I'd be.

When you neither walk nor talk
What mischief can you do?

Still, if someone came by
And said, "I hate this flower!"
I'd right off get mad and wilt.

Even if I were a flower
A proper child I'd never be...
Like a flower I'll never be.

お花だったら

もしも私がお花なら、
とてもいい子になれるだろ。

ものが言えなきゃ、あるけなきゃ、
なんでおいたをするものか。

だけど、誰かがやって来て、
いやな花だといったなら、
すぐに怒ってしぼむだろ。

もしもお花になったって、
やっぱしいい子にゃなれまいな、
お花のようにはなれまいな。

The Face on the Clock

A traveling salesman's bumbershoot,
It's short shadow in hand,
Goes down noon's blinding white street.

Right then I turn around....
Who's this white face
Watching me!?

I close my eyes, open them,
Take another look...
Clock's face it is.

Home alone and lonely
I stare long and hard...
But clock's face it stays.

時計の顔

旅あきうどのこうもりが、
みじかい影をつれてゆく、
白いまぶしいひるの路。

ふっとみかえりゃ誰かしら、
じっとみてます、
白い顔。

お目々つぶってまた開いて、
よく見りゃ
時計の顔でした。

おるす番ゆえ、さみしくて、
じっとみつめていたけれど、
それきり時計の顔でした。

Sunlight

The Sun's messengers
Together climbed the sky.
South Wind met them on the way
And asked, "Where to and why?"

One answered,
  "I cast light on earth
      So everyone can work."

One, pleased as punch,
  "I make flowers bloom
      So the world's a happy place."

One, sweet and gentle,
  "I hang the bridge
      The pure in spirit cross."

The last, looking friendless,
  "Oh, I just tag along
      To throw some shadows."

日の光

おてんと様のお使いが
揃って空をたちました。
みちで出逢ったみなみ風、
　（何しに、どこへ。）とききました。

一人は答えていいました。
　（この「明るさ」を地に撒くの、
みんなが仕事できるよう。）

一人はさもさも嬉しそう。
　（私はお花を咲かせるの、
世界をたのしくするために。）

一人はやさしく、おとなしく、
　（私は清いたましいの、
のぼる反り橋かけるのよ。）

残った一人はさみしそう。
　（私は「影」をつくるため、
やっぱり一しょにまいります。）

The Sad Princess

A brave prince saved the princess.
Home she came to her castle.

The castle of old, it is.
Roses bloom as once they did.

But the princess–Why so sad?–
Again today stares at the sky.

   "That witch was scary,
     But how I loved the days
     When I was a little bird.
     I spread my wings, gleaming white,
     And traveled, oh, so far
     Across the boundless sky."

Over the town drift petals.
At the castle the feast goes on.
But still the sad princess,
Alone at dusk in her garden,
Blind to her red, red roses,
Keeps on staring at the sky.

さみしい王女

つよい王子にすくわれて、
城へかえった、おひめさま。

城はむかしの城だけど、
薔薇もかわらず咲くけれど、

なぜかさみしいおひめさま、
きょうもお空を眺めてた。

　　（魔法つかいはこわいけど、
　　あのはてしないあお空を、
　　白くかがやく翅のべて、
　　はるかに遠く旅してた、
　　小鳥のころがなつかしい。）

街の上には花が飛び、
城に宴はまだつづく。
それもさみしいおひめさま、
ひとり日暮の花園で、
真紅な薔薇は見も向かず、
お空ばかりを眺めてた。

That Sail

When I looked at a shell
    up on the beach
That sail went away
    for good.

Just like that
    they went away.
There were people.
There were things.

帆

ちょいと
渚の貝がら見た間に、
あの帆はどっかへ
行ってしまった。

こんなふうに
行ってしまった、
誰かがあった——
何かがあった——

Spring Morning

Oh, the sparrows sing
And a fine day it is,
  Sleepy, sleepy,
    Sleepyhead.

Will the top eyelid open?
No, the bottom eyelid won't,
  Sleepy, sleepy,
    Sleepyhead.

春の朝

雀がなくな、
いい日和だな、
うっとり、うっとり
ねむいな。

上の瞼はあこうか、
下の瞼はまァだよ、
うっとり、うっとり
ねむいな。

Baby Leaves

"Nighty-night"
 Is the part the moon plays.
 He wraps you gently in his light
    and sings in silence a lullaby.

"Rise and shine"
 Is the part the wind plays.
 As the sky pales in the east
    she shakes you till you wake.

Your nursemaids during the day–
The songbirds.
They sometimes sing together, and sometimes
    hide up on a branch, then come out again.

Those little
Baby leaves
Suck their mother's milk and sleep,
    and while they sleep grow big.

葉っぱの赤ちゃん

「ねんねなさい」は
月の役。
そっと光りを着せかけて、
だまってうたうねんね唄。

「起っきなさい」は
風の役。
東の空のしらむころ、
ゆすっておめめさまさせる。

昼のお守りは
小鳥たち。
みんなで唄をうたったり、
枝にかくれて、また出たり。

ちいさな
葉っぱの赤ちゃんは、
おっぱいのんでねんねして、
ねんねした間にふとります。

Clover Leaf's Song

Where do my flowers go
When they get picked?

Here, there's blue sky.
Larks are singing.

But I wonder, too,
Where that happy wanderer
The wind's heading now.

Sweet little hands
Feel their way down flower stems.
Is one of them the hand
That'll pick me, you think?

げんげの葉の唄

花は摘まれて
どこへゆく

ここには青い空があり
うたう雲雀があるけれど

あのたのしげな旅びとの
風のゆくてが
おもわれる

花のつけ根をさぐってる
あの愛らしい手のなかに
私を摘む手は
ないかしら

Names of Flowers

I don't know the names of flowers
   other people know.

I know lots of names of flowers
   No one else knows.

You see, I gave them to them...
   Names I like to flowers I like.

The names for flowers people know
   Someone gave them, anyhow.

The sun alone, up in the sky,
   Knows what each name really is.

So I call them what I like.
   Just me....   Names I like....

草の名

人の知ってる草の名は、
私はちっとも知らないの。

人の知らない草の名を、
私はいくつも知ってるの。

それは私がつけたのよ、
好きな草には好きな名を。

人の知ってる草の名も、
どうせ誰かがつけたのよ。

ほんとの名まえを知ってるは、
空のお日さまばかりなの。

だから私はよんでるの、
私ばかりでよんでるの。

It's Weird

It's weird how
Shiny silver raindrops fall
    from black clouds.

It's weird how
Silkworms turn white
    when they eat green mulberry leaves.

It's weird how
Moonflowers open at dusk
    without a poke from anyone.

It's weird how
People I ask laugh and say,
    "Nothing strange in that."

不思議

私は不思議でたまらない、
黒い雲からふる雨が、
銀にひかっていることが。

私は不思議でたまらない、
青い桑の葉たべている、
蚕が白くなることが。

私は不思議でたまらない、
たれもいじらぬ夕顔が、
ひとりでぱらりと開くのが。

私は不思議でたまらない、
誰にきいても笑ってて、
あたりまえだ、ということが。

New Girl at School

The girl from away's
A cute girl,
So what can I do
To make us friends.

At noon recess
There she is
Leaning against
A cherry tree.

The girl from away
Talks like away,
So how should I say
What I say to her?

On the way home,
There she is,
And she's already
Got a friend.

転校生

よそから来た子は
かわいい子、
どうすりゃ、おつれに
なれよかな。

おひるやすみに
みていたら、
その子は桜に
もたれてた。

よそから来た子は
よそ言葉、
どんな言葉で
はなそかな。

かえりの路で
ふと見たら、
その子はお連れが
出来ていた。

Eyelash Rainbows

Rub, rub
And still they come.
In my tears
One thing I think:

Sure as sure
I'm adopted!

At the fringe of my lashes,
Pretty rainbows.
I look and I look and
One thing I think:

What snack'll be waiting
This afternoon?

睫毛の虹

ふいても、ふいても
湧いてくる、
涙のなかで
おもうこと。

　　——あたしはきっと、
　　　もらい児よ——

まつげのはしの
うつくしい、
虹を見い見い
おもうこと。

　　——きょうのお八つは、
　　　なにかしら——

Nanny's Story

That was the last time Nanny told it.
...And it's a story I like a lot.

"Heard that one before," I'd said.
She gave me a real sad look.

In Nanny's eyes I saw reflected,
Wildrose on a grassy hill.

I do miss that story so,
And, oh, if she'd just tell it
Five, no, ten times quietly I'd listen
And not once say a single word.

ばあやのお話

ばあやはあれきり話さない、
あのおはなしは、好きだのに。

「もうきいたよ」といったとき、
ずいぶんさびしい顔してた。

ばあやの瞳には、草山の、
野茨のはなが映ってた。

あのおはなしがなつかしい、
もしも話してくれるなら、
五度も、十度も、おとなしく、
だまって聞いていようもの。

Mama Walks on the Ocean

"Mama! Don't!
 That's the ocean there!
 See, here's the harbor.
 This chair's a boat
 About to sail away.
 So get in the boat!

"No, Mama, no...!
 Walk into the ocean
 And it's gluggity-glug!
 Don't just laugh.
 Hurry! Hurry and get in!"

Well, she went anyway.
But it's okay, you see,
Because my mama's special.
She can walk on the ocean.
She's special,
Really special.

海を歩く母さま

母さま、いやよ、
そこ、海なのよ。
ほら、ここ、港、
この椅子、お舟、
これから出るの。
お舟に乗ってよ。

あら、あら、だァめ、
海んなか歩いちゃ、
あっぷあっぷしてよ。
母さま、ほんと、
笑ってないで、
はよ、はよ、乗ってよ。

とうとう行っちゃった。
でも、でも、いいの、
うちの母さま、えらいの、
海、あるけるの。
えェらいな、
えェらいな。

To the Light

To the light!
To the light!

To where the sun shines through to
Even just one leaf...

Plants in the shade of bushes.

To the light!
To the light!

To where the candle burns,
Let wings be scorched...

Creatures flying in the night.

To the light!
To the light!

To where the sun beams down
On the biggest piece of ground...

Kids who live in town.

明るい方へ

明るい方へ
明るい方へ。

一つの葉でも
陽の洩るとこへ。

籔かげの草は。

明るい方へ
明るい方へ。

翅は焦げよと
灯のあるとこへ。

夜飛ぶ虫は。

明るい方へ
明るい方へ。

一分もひろく
日の射すとこへ。

都会に住む子等は。

Down This Road

I bet down this road
There's a big forest.
Hey, lone Sugarberry Tree,
Let's go down this road.

I bet down this road
There's a big ocean.
Hey, Froggie, in your lotus pond,
Let's go down this road.

I bet down this road
There's a big city.
Hey, Scarecrow, looking so sad,
Let's go down this road.

I bet down this road
Something special's waiting.
Hey, you all, let's get going.
Let's go down this road.

このみち

このみちのさきには、
大きな森があろうよ。
ひとりぼっちの榎よ、
このみちをゆこうよ。

このみちのさきには、
大きな海があろうよ。
蓮池のかえろよ、
このみちをゆこうよ。

このみちのさきには、
大きな都があろうよ。
さびしそうな案山子よ、
このみちを行こうよ。

このみちのさきには、
なにかなにかあろうよ。
みんなでみんなで行こうよ、
このみちをゆこうよ。

Sea's End

There where clouds rise,
Where rainbows root,

By boat, someday, I want to go,
Go to the end of the sea.

If it's too far, the sun sets,
And I can't see a single thing,

A pretty star I'll take in my hand,
Like I'd pick a red jujube.
Oh, let's go to the end of the sea.

海の果

雲の湧くのはあすこいら、
虹の根もともあすこいら。

いつかお舟でゆきたいな、
海の果までゆきたいな。

あまり遠くて、日が暮れて、
なにも見えなくなったって、

あかいなつめをもぐように、
きれいな星が手で採れる、
海の果までゆきたいな。

Sky-Blue Flowers

Listen close, you little flowers,
Color of the blue, blue sky.

Around here there used to be
A pretty black-eyed girl,
Always looking at the sky
Like I was just doing now.

Dawn to dusk the blue sky
Shining in her eyes,
They turned one day to little flowers
That even now watch the sky.

If what I say is right, why,
Flowers, you must know
More about the real true sky
Than wise professors do.

I'm always looking at the sky
And thinking lots and lots
But what's real and true I don't know.
I bet you see it all and do.

Wise flowers don't say a thing,
Just keep looking at the sky.
Those blue eyes, sky-dyed,
Still aren't tired of watching.

空いろの花

青いお空の色してる、
小さい花よ、よくお聴き。

むかし、ここらに黒い瞳の、
かわいい女の子があって、
さっき私のしてたよに、
いつもお空をみていたの。

一日青ぞら映るので、
お瞳はいつか、空いろの、
小さな花になっちゃって、
いまもお空をみているの。

花よ、わたしのお噺が、
もしもちがっていないなら、
おまえはえらい博士より、
ほんとの空を知っていよ。

いつも私が空をみて、
たくさん、たくさん、考えて、
ひとつもほんとは知らぬこと、
みんなみていよ、知っていよ。

えらいお花はだァまって、
じっとお空をみつめてる。
空に染まった青い瞳で、
いまも、飽きずにみつめてる。

The King Who Loved Gold

The king who loved gold,
His palace turned to gold.

Everything the king's hands touched,
Even the rose, was gold.

When the king's hands held her
His princess, too, was gold.

Where the king's hands reached
The whole world was gold.

Wait! Wait!
All that time
The sky stayed blue.

金のお好きな王さま

金のお好きな王さまの
御殿は金になりました。

王様のお手が触るとき、
薔薇ものこらず金でした。

王様のお手が抱くときに、
おひめさまさえ、金でした。

王様のお手のとどくとこ、
世界はみんな金でした。

けれども、けれども、
そのときに、
空はやっぱり青でした。

Laughs

They're a pretty rose color,
Smaller, maybe, than poppy seeds.
When they fall in the dirt
Great big flowers bloom
The way fireworks burst.

What a pretty sight to see
If laughs like these rolled out
The way tears well up.

わらい

それはきれいな薔薇いろで、
芥子つぶよりかちいさくて、
こぼれて土に落ちたとき、
ぱっと花火がはじけるように、
おおきな花がひらくのよ。

もしも泪がこぼれるように、
こんな笑いがこぼれたら、
どんなに、どんなに、きれいでしょう。

The Dewdrop

I won't tell a soul

That in a garden nook this morning
A flower spilled a tear,

Because if word gets around
And Honeybee hears

He'll go and give her nectar back
As if he'd done wrong.

露

誰にもいわずにおきましょう。

朝のお庭のすみっこで、
花がほろりと泣いたこと。

もしも噂がひろがって
蜂のお耳へはいったら、

わるいことでもしたように、
蜜をかえしに行くでしょう。

Telephone Pole

Gossipy sparrows twitter at his ears.
Telephone Pole wakes up.

When the greengrocers' carts have gone,
Then come workers stomping by.

Afternoon, a wind springs up,
Children press their ears to him.

A balloon, its string broken,
Brushes his nose and flies away.

Sunset, sundown, day is done,
Stars come out around his head.

The Salvation Army sings at his feet,
Telephone Pole nods off to sleep.

電信柱

耳もとでおしゃべり雀の声がして、
電信柱は眼がさめた。

野菜ぐるまの絶えたころ、
工夫がコツコツやって来た。

おひるすぎから風が出た、
子供がお耳をおっつけた。

糸を切られたふうせんは、
鼻をかすめて飛んでった。

夕焼小焼で日がくれた、
あたまの近くへ星が出た。

足もとで救世軍がうたうので、
電信柱はねむくなった。

A Dog

The day our dahlias bloomed
Blackie at the liquor shop died.

The lady there who gets angry
Every time we play in front
Was blubbering.

At school that day
I was telling it funny

And suddenly felt sad.

犬

うちのだりあの咲いた日に
酒屋のクロは死にました。

おもてであそぶわたしらを、
いつでも、おこるおばさんが、
おろおろ泣いて居りました。

その日、学校^{がくこ}でそのことを
おもしろそうに、話してて、

ふっとさみしくなりました。

Loquat Tree on the Mountain

Loquat on the mountain....
Someone I didn't know, up on a limb,
Threw to us climbing the pass
A bunch, branch and all:
   Ripe, yellow
     loquat fruits!

Loquat on the mountain....
This time, just leaves; no one here.
Blown along by an autumn wind,
Down from the pass I come:
   How long
     one shadow can be!

山の枇杷

山の枇杷、
知らない人が枝にいて、
峠をのぼるわたしらに
枝ごと投げてくれました。
　　黄いろく熟れた
　　枇杷の実を——

山の枇杷、
いまは葉ばかり、誰もいず、
峠のみちのあき風に
吹かれて私はくだります。
　　ひとつの影の
　　ながいこと——

Is That an Echo?

If I say, "Let's play,"
"Let's Play," comes back.

If I say, "Stupid!"
"Stupid!" comes back.

If I say, "I'm not playing anymore!"
"Not playing anymore!" comes back.

Then afterwards
When I start feeling sad,

"Sorry, yeh," I say and
"Sorry, yeh," comes back.

Is that an echo?
No....not anybody.

こだまでしょうか

「遊ぼう」っていうと
「遊ぼう」っていう。

「馬鹿」っていうと
「馬鹿」っていう。

「もう遊ばない」っていうと
「遊ばない」っていう。

そうして、あとで
さみしくなって、

「ごめんね」っていうと
「ごめんね」っていう。

こだまでしょうか、
いいえ、誰でも。

AFTERWORD

KANEKO Misuzu cast a wise and gentle gaze that reached around the globe, across countries and cultures, bringing to her verses which she wrote down for the ages.

It has long been my dream that people in lands beyond these shores might one day hear the songs she sang, and so I asked D. P. Dutcher to put them in English.

He read and he read until his heart was full and then he rendered some sixty of her sweet, deep poems.

The occasional rhyme, echoes of the original seven-five meter, and spare diction have issued in a text that is equally accessible to child and adult — I even find myself singing snatches.

It is my fond hope that Mother Goose, who has winged her way into the hearts of generations of English-speaking children, will soar off into the sunset with *Something Nice* in her wicker basket and sing these songs of peace in far lands to ears young and old.

YAZAKI Setsuo

あとがき

　金子みすゞのまなざしは、時代を越え、国家や民族や宗教を越え、人類が共通に求めてきた英知のまなざしといっていいでしょう。

　このみすゞの作品を私たちだけでなく、世界中の人に読んでもらえたらと願い、今回、みすゞを愛する翻訳家、D.P.ダッチャーさんに翻訳をお願いしました。

　ダッチャーさんは、ミューズがほほえんでくれるまで、みすゞの作品で心をいっぱいにし、みすゞの平易で、深い日本語を、美しい英語にうつしかえてくれました。

　そればかりか、おとなだけでなく子どもにも読んでもらえるようにと、ことばを選んでくださったおかげで、わたしにでも口ずさめる、みごとに韻をふんだ、リズムのある、現代のマザーグースになりました。

　この『サムシング・ナイス』を通して、日本の母・金子みすゞを、世界のマザーグースとして、みんなが口ずさんでくれたらいいな、そして、だれもが倖せな二十一世紀であるといいなぁと心から思います。

矢崎節夫

Translator's Note

The Japanese poet KANEKO Misuzu was born on 11 April 1903 in Senzaki, a fishing port in southwestern Honshu facing on the Sea of Japan. Her career as a writer of poetry for children began in earnest at the age of twenty shortly after she became the manager and sole employee of a small bookstore in Shimonoseki, a town at the southern tip of Honshu. Here she discovered a clutch of magazines which were riding the crest of a boom in children's literature and which solicited stories and verse from their readers.

Kaneko sent in a number of poems, five of which, among them "The Fishes", were separately accepted for publication in the September 1923 issue of four of these magazines. Over the next five years she published fifty-one more verses. The sixty-four poems in this selection have been drawn from among five hundred and twelve verses written, in Kaneko's own hand, in three notebooks which were brought to light in 1982, half a century after her death, by Mr. YAZAKI Setsuo. Kaneko Misuzu's short but keenly lived life came to a close on 10 March 1930. She was twenty-six years old.

D. P. Dutcher

訳者注

　日本の詩人金子みすゞは明治36年4月11日に、日本海に面する山口県の漁港仙崎に生まれた。童謡詩人としての活動は20歳の時に、本州の最南端にある下関市の小さな本屋の店長兼唯一の従業員となったころに始まった。ここで、読者から短編や詩歌を募集し、児童文学のブームに乗っていたいくつかの雑誌と出会った。みすゞが数編の詩を投稿し、そのうち「お魚」を含む5編が別々に4つの雑誌の大正12年9月号に掲載された。これから5年間にわたってさらに51編を発表した。本選集にある64編の詩は彼女の死後50年を経て、昭和57年に矢崎節夫氏によって発見されたみすゞ自筆の3冊の手帳に収められた512編の詩から選んだ。短くはあったが、ひたむきに生きたみすゞの一生は昭和5年3月10日に閉じられた。享年26歳であった。

　　　　　　　　　　　　　　D.P.ダッチャー

◎訳者略歴

D. P. Dutcher／Translator; editor of dictionaries. Born in 1944 in New York, USA. Received B.A. and M.A. degrees from the University of Hawaii. Studied for a doctoral degree in classical Japanese literature at Harvard University. He is an editor of several English-Japanese and Japanese-English dictionaries, including *The Kenkyusha Dictionary of English Collocations,* and has done translations from both classical and modern Japanese. The CD-ROM *GADGET* was widely acclaimed in the U.S.

D.P.ダッチャー／翻訳家、辞書編纂者。1944年、アメリカのニューヨーク州に生まれる。ハワイ大学卒業。同大学修士。ハーバード大学博士課程修了（日本古典文学専攻）。Collier's百科事典（マクミラン社）の日本文化に関する大項目のほか、日本語・日本文学についての著述がある。『新編 英和活用大辞典』（研究社）などの英和・和英辞典の編集委員を務めるほか、古典から現代まで幅広い翻訳を手がけている。CD-ROM *GADGET*（シナジー幾何学）は全米で話題を呼んだ。

改訂新版　金子みすゞ童謡集 Something Nice サムシング ナイス

詩　金子みすゞ／訳　D.P.ダッチャー

あとがき————矢崎節夫
企画・プロデュース——徳永青也
制作協力————高橋豊子
◉
発行日————2019年9月　第1刷発行
発行者————飯田聡彦
発行所————JULA出版局
　　　　　　〒113-8611東京都文京区本駒込6-14-9 フレーベル館内
　　　　　　TEL.03-5395-6657
発売元————株式会社フレーベル館
　　　　　　〒113-8611東京都文京区本駒込6-14-9 TEL.03-5395-6637
印刷所————新日本印刷株式会社
製本所————小高製本工業株式会社
カバー装画——瀬藤優
デザイン・装丁——三上眞佐子

148P　22×16cm　NDC911　ISBN978-4-577-61002-2

＊金子みすゞの詩は、『金子みすゞ全集』より転載。表記は旧仮名づかい・旧漢字を新しいものに改め、ルビは一部省略している。
＊落丁・乱丁本はお取り替えいたします。